Chirp Chirp Cha-Ree! More Great Mathemachicken books for you!

1: Hide and Go Beak

2: Have a Slice Day

The Great MATHEMACHICKEN
Sing High, Sing Crow

NANCY KRULIK
Illustrated by CHARLIE ALDER

PIXEL+INK

PIXEL+INK

Text copyright © 2024 by Nancy Krulik
Illustrations copyright © 2024 by Charlie Alder
All rights reserved

Pixel+Ink is an imprint of TGM Development Corp.
www.pixelandinkbooks.com
Printed and bound in December 2023 at Toppan Leefung, DongGuan, China.
Book design by Katrina Damkoehler and Amy Toth

Library of Congress Cataloging-in-Publication Data
Names: Krulik, Nancy E., author. | Alder, Charlie, illustrator.
Title: Sing high, sing crow / Nancy Krulik ; illustrated by Charlie Alder.
Description: First edition. | New York : Pixel+Ink, 2024. | Series: The great mathemachicken ; book 3 | Audience: Ages 5–8. | Audience: Grades 2-3. | Summary: Chirpy the chick learns that music is math and songs can solve noisy problems.
Identifiers: LCCN 2023025749 | ISBN 9781645952022 (hardcover)
Subjects: CYAC: Chickens—Fiction. | Birds—Fiction. | Noise—Fiction. | Music--Fiction. | Mathematics—Fiction. | Problem solving—Fiction. | LCGFT: Animal fiction.
Classification: LCC PZ7.K9416 Si 2024 | DDC [Fic]—dc22
LC record available at https://.loc.gov/2023025749

Hardcover ISBN: 978-1-64595-202-2
E-book ISBN: 978-1-64595-204-6

First Edition

1 3 5 7 9 10 8 6 4 2

For Ian, who writes music that
makes his mom sing —N.K.

The author would like to thank Basil Wright;
Stephen Krulik, EdD; and Amanda Burwasser
for their assistance with this story.

For J & W, the cutest chickens in the coop xo
—C.A.

Contents

1. Be Quiet! 1

2. WAKE UP! 12

3. Alarm *Cluck*! 16

4. Something Strange 19

5. La La La . . . *Quack* 23

6. Feathers Get in the Way 32

7. *Zzzz* 38

8. Shoop! Shoop! *Swoop*! 42

9. I've Got a Head-*egg*! 50

10. Can Chickens Sing? 56

11. Sing High, Sing Low.
    Sing *Eggs*-tra Quiet! 61

12. Chirp Chirp Cha-Ree!
    Sing with Me! 68

13. *Cheep* Trick 74

14. Cock-a-Doodle-Doo 84

1
Be Quiet!

♪ *FEATHERS TICKLE*

FEATHERS FLY

BUT I'VE GOT A FEATHER IN MY EYE! ♪

Chirpy curled up in a tight little ball. She covered her ears with her wings.

But nothing she did blocked out the noise of the crows singing their song up in the tree.

♪ *THIS FEATHER ITCHES*
IT MAKES ME CRY
FEATHERS DON'T BELONG INSIDE
YOUR EYE ♪

It was dark in the coop. But the chickens were wide awake.

♪ *THIS FEATHER MAKES MY EYE RAW*
CAW! CAW! CAW! ♪

No one could sleep through that.

"Be quiet up there!" the rooster, Sir Wattles, shouted to the crows. "Don't you know it's nighttime?"

"We're having band practice," one of the crows answered him. "Rock 'n' roll band practices are loud."

"And they're at night," another added.

"I don't care what you crows are doing," Sir Wattles told them. "I just want it to stop."

"If you chickens knew anything, you'd know we aren't all *crows*," the biggest bird said.

"We're all in the same *family* of birds," one of the blue-and-white birds explained. "That's why we call ourselves the Crow Family Band."

"This is our big song," the magpie told the chickens. "You're lucky you get to hear us play it live."

♪ *THIS FEATHER MAKES MY EYE RAW CAW! CAW! CAW!* ♪

"I can't take it anymore," Clucky grumbled. "That noise has to stop."

"Oh man," one of the crows groaned.

"Did he just say what I thought he did?" added another.

A blue jay swooped angrily to the ground and stared Clucky in the eye.

"Did you just call our song *noise*?"

"Yes, I did," Clucky replied. "You sound terrible."

"That's the worst thing anyone could ever say to a musician. Boy, are you gonna be sorry you said it," the blue jay warned Clucky.

"Oh yeah?" Clucky clucked angrily.

He picked up an acorn and threw it at the blue jay.

But the jay was quick. He flew back up into the tree.

Chirpy frowned.

She would never throw an acorn at anyone.

She used *math and science* to solve problems in the coop.

Still, Clucky had managed to quiet the crows.

Now the chickens in the coop could sleep.

Or maybe not.

The crows were pelting the chickens with acorns.

Clucky had made them really mad.

"It's easier to throw things down than it is to toss them up," a crow said.

That was true. Chirpy had learned all about it in school.

A force called *gravity* helped pull things toward the ground. That was why things fell.

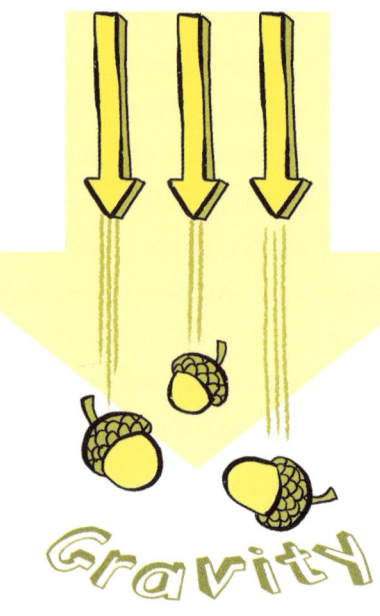

That was a lot of gravity at work.

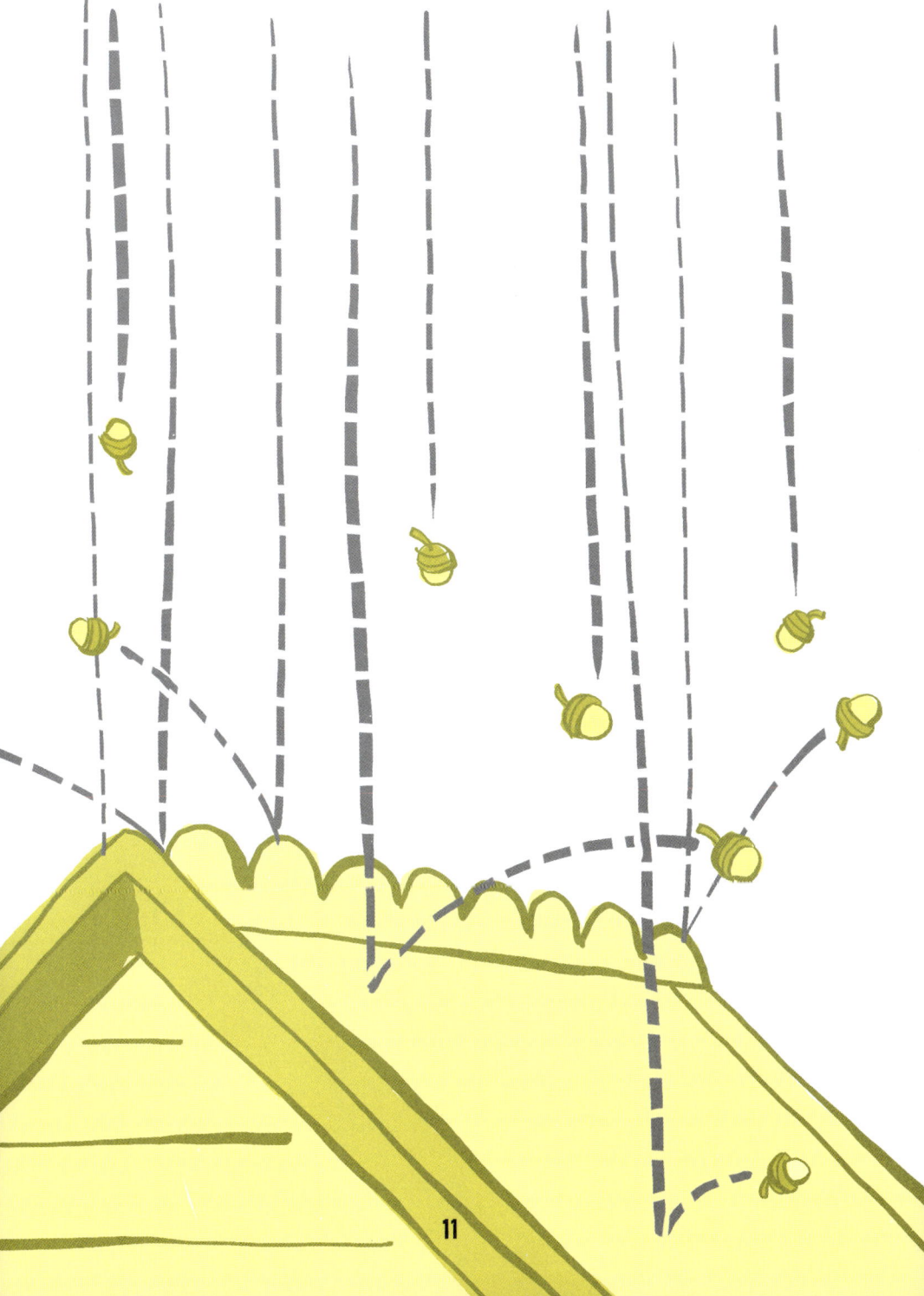

WAKE UP!

♪ *Wake up! Wake up! Wake up!* ♪

Chirpy's eyes popped open.

The crow family had finally stopped throwing acorns into the coop.

So Chirpy had been able to fall asleep.

At least for a little while.

But now the whole crow family was singing again.

And this song was louder than the one they were singing last night.

WAKE UP! WAKE UP! WAKE UP!
The sky may still be dark
And the sun not rising
But we crows are awake
Which should not be surprising!
Don't you wait for the rooster
And his cock-a-doodle-doo
Be-caws it's time for you to stir
And what we say you'll do
WAKE UP! WAKE UP! WAKE UP!
We will play what we want
It's your ears that need fixin'
The song's here to taunt
And we don't do remixin'
WAKE UP! WAKE UP! WAKE UP!

"What do you think you're doing?" Clucky shouted up into the treetop.

"We told you you'd be sorry for calling our song *noise*," the magpie reminded him.

"This is our *new* song," one of the crows added. "How do you chickens like it?"

Alarm Cluck!

Grrr . . .

Chirpy really did not like waking up before the rooster's call.

The rooster was not happy, either.

"It's *my* job to wake everyone," Sir Wattles grumbled. "There's only room for one alarm *cluck* in this coop!"

"Chirpy, you've got to do something," Squawky pleaded.

"We need you. You're the Great Mathemachicken," Shelly said. "Our superhero."

"At least I *tried* to stop them from making noise," Clucky boasted.

"All you did was make things worse," Squawky said.

"I'm going back to sleep after breakfast," Buck-Buck said.

"Me, too," Shelly agreed.

"Me, three," Squawky added.

Chirpy wouldn't have time for a nap. She had to go to school.

After all, she never knew what she might learn in Mrs. Zoober's class.

Maybe something to help make things in the coop less noisy tonight.

Something Strange

"Stay awake," Chirpy whispered to herself. "Stay awake."

Chirpy was *so* tired.

But she just couldn't fall asleep in Mrs. Zoober's classroom.

Even though she and her friend

Quackers had found the perfect place to hide.

They could see Mrs. Zoober. But she could not see them.

Mrs. Zoober stood in the front of the classroom.

The kids all sat up in their chairs.

Chirpy sat up tall, too.

She couldn't wait to hear what Mrs. Zoober was going to teach them today.

"Is everyone excited to start the day with Ms. Mezzo's music class?" Mrs. Zoober asked the children. "Let's line up and go to the music room."

The kids cheered.

But Chirpy wasn't happy at all.

She wanted to learn more math and science.

Those were the subjects that helped her solve problems at the coop.

Not something strange called *music*.

5
La la la . . . Quack

♪

It's time to learn a happy song
One where we can sing along
Music class is so much fun
A joyful place for everyone
La la la la

♪

Ms. Mezzo sang as the class came into the music room.

This was not an angry song like the one that had woken everyone in the coop.

This was a happy song.

Chirpy saw the kids were singing along.

Well, most of them, anyway.

A shy girl in the back tapped her foot instead of singing.

Chirpy did not sing, either.

Chickens weren't allowed in school, so Chirpy had to hide and be very, very quiet.

Quackers was supposed to be

quiet, too, but he could not help himself.

"*La la la . . . quack!*"

"Shhh . . . ," Chirpy warned.

"Today, we are going to learn about *rhythm*," Ms. Mezzo told the class.

"What's that?" a girl asked.

"*Rhythm* is the way long-lasting notes and short-lasting notes are put together in a pattern to make a song," Ms. Mezzo explained.

Ms. Mezzo pointed to a picture on the wall.

"Hey! That looks like a big, white duck egg!" Quackers exclaimed.

Chirpy had been thinking the same thing.

Except about a *chicken* egg.

"This is a whole note," Ms. Mezzo told the class. "It lasts for four beats."

"I don't get it," one boy called out.

Chirpy was glad he had said that.

She didn't understand what Ms. Mezzo meant, either.

Ms. Mezzo smiled. "Let's try this. I will sing a whole note. And you clap four times."

"*La-a-a-a*," Ms. Mezzo sang a long note.

One. Two. Three. Four. The kids clapped as she sang.

"Very good," Ms. Mezzo said.

She pointed to a picture of two smaller white eggs with sticks on them.

"These are half notes," the teacher said. "Each one lasts for two beats. Two is half of four."

Ms. Mezzo sang a note that

 lasted half as long as the whole note. *"La-a."*

One. Two. The kids clapped as she sang.

Ms. Mezzo pointed to one more picture. It looked like four small black eggs with sticks attached.

Chirpy had never seen eggs like those before.

"These are quarter notes. Each note lasts for just one beat. One is one-fourth of four," Ms. Mezzo explained. "We call one-fourth a quarter."

The teacher sang a quick note. *"La."*

One. The kids clapped one time as she sang.

"I've heard *whole*, *half*, and *quarter* before," Quackers said. "But where, I wonder?"

"Those are *fractions*," Chirpy told Quackers. "We learned about them in Mrs. Zoober's class."

"Oh right," Quackers replied. "The kids each ate one slice of pizza from the pie. Those were eighths. And we got to eat the leftover crusts. *Mmm.* Fractions are delicious."

Suddenly, Chirpy started jumping up and down *eggs*-citedly.

She'd just realized something really *Zoober*.

Fractions were math! Which meant . . .

6
Feathers Get in the Way

"Let's play with pitch while we sing," Ms. Mezzo told the kids.

Chirpy cocked her head.

Pitch?

She'd never heard of that.

"Remember, pitch is how low

or high a note sounds," Ms. Mezzo explained.

Chirpy ruffled her feathers.

She didn't understand.

The teacher pointed to the kids on one side of the room. "You will sing the low parts in the song," she told them. "Low notes sound like a lion roaring."

Well, that didn't help. Chirpy had never heard a lion roar.

She didn't even know what a lion was.

"Let's try it," Ms. Mezzo said.

"*It's time to learn a happy song,*" the kids on that side of the room sang.

Oh, now Chirpy understood.

The kids singing the low parts sounded like Sir Wattles, with his deep rooster voice.

Ms. Mezzo turned to the kids on the other side of the room.

"Now you will sing the high parts," she told them. "High notes sound like a dolphin's cry."

Chirpy wasn't sure what the teacher meant by that.

Neither was Quackers.

"I wonder, what's a dolphin?" he whispered. "And I wonder, why is it sad?"

Chirpy shrugged.

She had no idea.

The kids on that side of the room began to sing the high part.

They sounded a little bit squeaky, like the just-hatched chicks that went *cheep, cheep, cheep.*

Now Chirpy understood.

The class clapped along with the lengths of the notes.

Long whole notes.

One. Two. Three. Four.

Faster half notes.

One. Two.

And even faster quarter notes.

One. One. One. One.

The clapping made a happy, snappy noise. Chirpy liked it.

She and Quackers tried to clap, too, but their wings didn't make a sound.

"Our wings don't make noise when we clap," Chirpy whispered. "The feathers are too soft."

"Do you know which side of a duck has the *most* feathers?" Quackers asked her.

Chirpy shook her head.

"The outside!" Quackers laughed so hard he fell over. "I really *quack* myself up."

Chirpy laughed, too. She was much happier now.

Music class was so much fun, just like the song said.

Zzzz...

"Today was a really great day!" Quackers told Chirpy as they rode the school bus home. "I like music class."

"Me, too," Chirpy said with a yawn.

"I wonder how many different kinds of songs there are?" Quackers asked.

"I don't know," Chirpy answered. "Lots and lots, I guess."

As the bus rolled along, Chirpy hummed a little song.

It wasn't a happy song like the kids sang in music class.

Or a loud, angry song like the Crow Family Band sang to wake the chickens.

This was a slow, sleepy song.

Because Chirpy was feeling slow and sleepy.

"That's very nice," Quackers told Chirpy. "It's soft like the lullaby my mama sings when . . . *Zzzz.*"

Quackers stopped quacking.

Right in the middle of his sentence.

Chirpy's slow, sleepy song had put him to sleep.

Hey! Wait a minute!

Chirpy had a *Zoober* idea!

Well, actually, it was a *Mezzo* idea.

"I've got it!" Chirpy shouted *eggs*-citedly.

Quackers blinked his eyes open and stared at her.

"I wonder what you're talking about?" he asked sleepily.

"I know how to quiet the Crow Family Band!" she cheered. "And you helped me figure it out. Thanks, Quackers!"

"You are welcome." Quackers closed his eyes again. "Wake me when we get home, okay?"

8

Shoop! Shoop! Swoop!

"I've got it!" Chirpy shouted *eggs-citedly* as she ran into the coop.

"Be quiet!" Clucky grumbled at her. "I'm trying to get some rest."

"I think I've figured out a way to keep the crow family quiet tonight!"

Chirpy told him.

"You *think*?" Clucky rolled over. "I'm going back to sleep."

But the other chickens were wide awake.

"Can you really make them stop singing?" Shelly asked.

"Of course she can," Squawky answered. "After all, she's the Great Mathemachicken."

Just then, the birds in the tree began to flap their wings.

They wiggled their tail feathers.

And danced from side to side.

Then they began to sing a new song.

Shoop shoop

Shoop shoop

Shoop . . .

"Will you guys cut it out," Clucky shouted up into the tree. "How's a chicken supposed to nap with all that noise?"

"You can't please that chicken," the raven complained. "We're practicing during the day, and he's still complaining."

"And he called our music noise, *again,*" the magpie grumbled.

"I guess I'm gonna have to fly down there and remind him how much we hate that," one of the two jays said angrily. He turned to his bandmates. "Okay, guys. Sing me down there!"

The Crow Family Band began singing again.

Shoop shoop
Shoop shoop
Shoop . . .
SWOOP!

"I warned you about calling our music . . . ," the jay began.

Then he noticed something hiding behind a big rock.

"Whoa!" the blue jay exclaimed. "Did anyone know there was a pile of food here?"

"Hey!" Clucky shouted. "I was saving those seeds for a snack!"

"You took extra food?" Squawky asked Clucky angrily. "No fair!"

"Clucky!" Atilla the Hen scolded. "We talked about sharing. So, I'm *sure* you were planning on sharing that feed."

"Um . . . yeah," Clucky told his mom. "Of course I was."

"Don't mind if I do." The blue jay grabbed a giant beakful of feed. "Thanks for sharing!"

Clucky stared at the other chickens.

The other chickens glared back at Clucky.

They didn't believe he had really meant to share.

Clucky *never* shared.

"Don't be mad at me!" Clucky insisted. "Be mad at Chirpy. She's the one who said she could stop the crows from bothering us. And she didn't."

The chickens all turned their glares toward Chirpy.

Uh-oh.

9
I've Got a Head-*egg*!

Chirpy scribbled musical notes in the dirt.

She scratched them out.

And scribbled some more.

Writing music was hard.

"What are those?" Buck-Buck asked.

"Musical notes," Chirpy told her. "I learned about them in school."

"School!" Clucky grumbled. "That's all you talk about."

"School is where I learn math and science," Chirpy explained.

"That's what makes her the Great Mathemachicken," Squawky told Clucky.

"Chirpy," Sir Wattles called. "If you're going to get rid of those crows, do it before the sun sets and they start making those awful noises again."

Chirpy's mother hopped over.

"How's it going?" she asked.

Chirpy frowned. "I don't know which is worse. The crows singing or the chicks clucking."

Chirpy's mom wrapped her wing around her daughter's shoulders and gave her a hug.

"I bet my little girl could work faster if you all left her alone," she told the others.

Chirpy smiled up at her mother. "Thanks."

"You're welcome. But please hurry and solve this mess soon. Those crows are giving me a head-*egg*."

10

Can Chickens Sing?

"Shhhh . . ." Squawky hissed at the other chickens in the coop.

"Chirpy is finally going to tell us her plan," Shelly added.

"It had better be a good one," Sir Wattles grumbled.

"We're going to sing our *own* song," Chirpy told them.

The chicks stared at Chirpy.

Then they stared at one another.

And then they shook their heads.

"That's just going to make *more* noise in the coop," Clucky pointed out.

He smiled proudly. There was nothing Clucky liked more than when Chirpy was wrong.

But Chirpy wasn't wrong.

At least she *hoped* she wasn't.

"We're going to sing a *soft* song," she explained. "The crow family will have to be quiet if they want to hear us."

Atilla the Hen spread her giant wings wide. "What makes you think they're going to *want* to hear our song?"

"The crow family loves music," Chirpy replied. "I'm hoping they'll want to hear a different kind of song."

Atilla the Hen shook her big chicken head.

"Even if that's true, it will only keep them quiet until the song is over," she told Chirpy. "Then they'll go right back to making more noise."

"Not if we sing them a quiet, peaceful song that puts them to sleep," Chirpy explained.

"It's never going to work," Clucky told the others.

"Why not?" Chirpy asked.

Clucky puffed out his chest. "Because we don't know any songs."

"That's okay. I wrote one for us," Chirpy told him.

"I guess it's worth a try," Shelly said.

"It can't hurt," Squawky agreed.

"It could even be fun," Buck-Buck added. "Maybe."

"It will be," Chirpy assured her. "You'll see."

11

Sing High, Sing Low, Sing *Eggs*-tra Quiet!

"Okay, I'm going to teach you the song," Chirpy told the others. "It has whole notes, half notes, and quarter notes. Try and follow the rhythm."

Chirpy would have loved to explain all that to her friends.

She really liked talking about math.

Just not now.

The sun was going down.

Pretty soon the Crow Family Band would start practicing.

If the chicks were going to get any sleep tonight, they had to learn her song now.

"Just sing along with me," she told the others. "And make sure to sing *eggs*-tra quiet."

♪ *This is a bird world lullaby*
Rest your soft, feathery head
It's no time for wings to fly
You need to go to . . . ♪

Chirpy stopped singing and shook her head.

"Why did you stop?" Shelly asked.

"We were having fun!" Squawky added.

The chickens may have been having fun, but they weren't making very good music.

They had trouble following Chirpy as she sang.

"Someone is singing the wrong rhythm," she told the others.

"It's Clucky," Squawky said.

"He's singing the whole song wrong," Shelly pointed out.

"And he's very loud," Sir Wattles added. "No one should be louder than a rooster."

Clucky shook his head so hard, one of his feathers flew off.

"My singing isn't wrong," he said. "The *song* is what's wrong."

Chirpy took a deep breath.

There had to be a way to stop Clucky from ruining the song.

Suddenly, Chirpy remembered the shy little girl in Ms. Mezzo's class.

She hadn't been singing at all, just tapping her feet.

"Clucky, I have a special part for you," Chirpy said. "Instead of singing, I want you to clap your wings together like this."

Chirpy clapped her wings.

Clucky gave her a strange look.

"Why should I do that?" he asked. "You can barely hear it."

Hmmm . . . Chirpy wasn't sure how to answer that without making Clucky mad.

"Because . . . ," Chirpy said slowly as she thought. "That way the crow family will have to be *eggs*-tra quiet just to hear *you*."

Clucky cocked his head and thought.

Finally, he bragged, "That means I will be the one to make them the *most* quiet."

Chirpy clamped her beak shut tight to keep from *cracking* up.

Clucky had fallen for it.

"*Eggs*-actly," she told him.

12

Chirp Chirp Cha-Ree! Sing with Me!

"Chirp chirp cha-ree! Sing with me!" Chirpy called to the other chickens.

She tapped her foot on the ground to make a rhythm.

Then the chickens began to sing.

♪ This is a bird world lullaby
Rest your soft, feathery head
It's no time for wings to fly
You need to go to bed ♪

Chirpy looked up at the crow family.

They were whispering to each other.

They weren't listening to the chickens at all.

Oh no!

Chirpy's plan didn't seem to be working.

But the Great Mathemachicken wasn't about to give up.

She'd worked too hard on this song to stop now.

Besides, she didn't *eggs*-actly have any other *Zoober* ideas to quiet the crows.

♪ *Sing the quarter notes fast*
Cheep cheep cheep cheep
Sing the whole notes slooooow
Cheeeeeeeep
You're getting sleepy at last
Off to dreamland you go
When in the sky you see the moon
It's time for you to sing it
Even if you don't know the tune
It's okay to wing it ♪

Sing the quarter notes fast

Cheep cheep cheep cheep

Sing the whole notes slooooow

Cheeeeeeeep

You're getting sleepy at last

Off to dreamland you go

In the morning we'll sing again
For now, though, please don't blow it
Rooster, crow, chick, and hen
Will sleep before we know it

13

Cheep Trick

"Hey! That song's not bad!" one of the crows exclaimed as the chickens finished their song.

Chirpy took a little bow.

"Thank you," she said. "I just wrote it. Do you want to hear us sing it again?"

She really hoped they did.

The crows had almost fallen asleep the first time.

One more lullaby would surely do the trick.

"I was thinking *we* could give it a try," the biggest crow said. "Because we're a *real* band."

That made Chirpy angry.

"We're a real band, too," she insisted.

"Oh yeah?" the magpie asked her. "Then what's your band name?"

"Every *real* band has a name," one of the blue jays added.

"How about Clucky and the Other Ones?" Clucky suggested.

Oh no. There was no way Chirpy was letting THAT happen.

Cheep. Cheep. Cheep.

Chirpy could hear other chickens trying to come up with band names, too.

But Chirpy was the one who should come up with the name.

After all, she'd been the one who had come up with a way to *trick* the crows into sleeping.

That was it! Chirpy hopped up and down *eggs*-citedly.

"Our band name is Cheep Trick!"

"I like it!" Sir Wattles exclaimed.

"Me, too!" Chirpy's mother's friend, Princess Lay-a, added.

"Cheep Trick, it is!" Atilla the Hen cheered.

Clucky looked at her with surprise.

"But, Mama," he said. "What about the band name *I* came up with?"

"When you write a song, you can name your own band," she told him.

"And now that we're a real band, *we* should be the ones to sing Chirpy's song again," Sir Wattles announced.

"If we want to sing your song, we're gonna sing it," the raven insisted.

"Yeah!" the magpie agreed. "And we'll sing it *our* way."

♪ **THIS IS A BIRD WORLD LULLABY!** ♪

The Crow Family Band were practically shouting.

Chirpy covered her ears.

"That's not the way you sing a lullaby," she told them.

"Who says?" one of the crows demanded.

"Everybody," Chirpy said. "You always sing a lullaby softly."

The raven started banging his sticks on the tree again.

The other birds in the tree opened their mouths wide to belt out the song.

Oh no! Everything was going wrong.

"How about we all sing the new song *together*," Chirpy suggested. "One big bird band."

The crow family birds whispered to one another.

"Just try singing softly," Chirpy added. "It's fun to try doing something new."

"We're not singing *cheep, cheep, cheep*," one of the crows told Chirpy.

"We can leave that part out," Chirpy agreed.

The Crow Family Band went back to whispering.

Chirpy waited nervously down below for an answer.

Finally, the big raven nodded his head.

"Okay, Cheep Trick," he told the chickens. "Let's all have a *caw*-ncert!"

♪ "This is a bird world lullaby," Chirpy began.

"Rest your soft, feathery head...," the Crow Family Band and Cheep Trick joined in.

Some birds sang the high part.

Some birds sang the low part.

Clucky sang *no* part.

They were all having a fun time making music together.

Best of all, everyone—even the birds in the crow family—was getting really, really sleepy.

♪ *In the morning we'll sing again.*

For now, though, please don't blow it

*Rooster, crow, chick, and hen
Will sleep before . . . Zzzzzzzzz* ♪

14
Cock-a-Doodle-Doo

"Cock-a-doodle-doo!"

Chirpy pulled her head out from under her wing.

She looked at the sunrise and smiled.

She'd slept all night.

And woken to the rooster's call.

One by one, the other chicks in the coop began to awaken.

"Well, goodbye, chickens!" the magpie called down to the coop.

"It was fun jamming with you!" a crow added.

"Where are you going?" Chirpy asked them. "I thought you liked this spot for practicing."

"We do," a blue jay answered. "But we're taking the Crow Family Band out on tour."

"Yeah," a crow agreed. "There are a whole lot of different birds we can sing with."

Chirpy was sad the Crow Family Band was leaving.

It had been fun singing with them.

She waved to each bird as they flew off.

Two blue jays.

One raven.

One magpie.

Three crows.

"What are you doing?" Shelly asked Chirpy.

"Counting crows," Chirpy said. "I like counting."

"You'd better stop counting and get moving if you want to go to school today," Chirpy's mother reminded her.

Of course, Chirpy wanted to go to school today.

Just then, Chirpy heard the school bus honking as it came down the street.

Honk! Honk!

The sound was music to her ears.

Make Your Own Paper Plate Tambourine

You can keep the beat with a tambourine you make all by yourself.

Here's what you need:

2 small (6- or 7-inch) paper plates

5 craft jingle bells

Hole punch

5 twist ties

Tempera paint

Stickers

Glitter glue

A grown-up to help

Here's what you do:

1) Place the two plates face-to-face, making sure the edges match up.

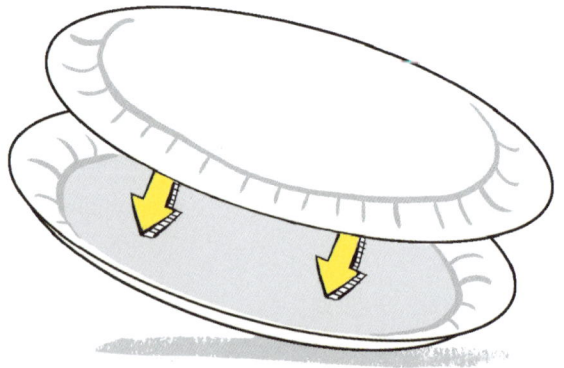

2) Ask your grown-up to punch five holes, evenly spaced, around the edges of the two plates.

3) Paint the bottom sides of the plates any way you like.

4) Allow the paint to dry. Then use the stickers and glitter glue to decorate the painted sides of the plates.

5) String a jingle bell onto the middle of the twist tie. Bend the ends of the twist tie toward each another.

6) Repeat Step 5 for each of the bells.

7) Put the plates together so the painted sides face out and the punched holes line up perfectly.

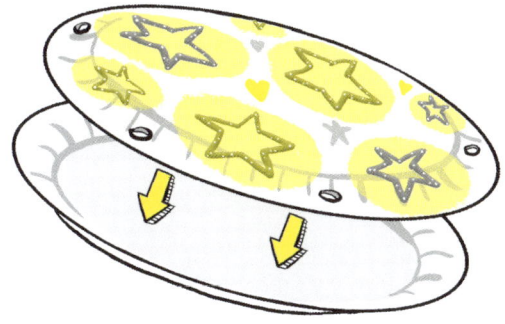

8) To attach the first bell, slip one end of the twist tie through one of the pairs of lined-up holes on the plates. Twist the ends together tightly.

9) Repeat Step 8 four times until all five bells are firmly attached to the paper plates.

Your tambourine is ready to play!

See how Chirpy became the Great Mathemachicken!

Can a new friend and pizza help Chirpy solve trouble in the coop?

NANCY KRULIK is the international bestselling author of more than two hundred books for children. Her series, including Katie Kazoo, Switcheroo; George Brown, Class Clown; Magic Bone; Princess Pulverizer; and Ms. Frogbottom's Field Trips, are beloved around the world. She lives in New York City.

CHARLIE ALDER has written and illustrated many books for children, including *Daredevil Duck* and *Chicken Break!* When not drawing chickens, Charlie can be found in her studio drinking coffee, arranging her crayons, and inventing more accidental animal heroes. She lives in Devon, England.